NANCY DREW

#9 girl detective ®

Ghost In The Machinery

STEFAN PETRUCHA • Writer

SHO MURASE • Artist

with 3D CG elements by CARLOS JOSE GUZMAN

Based on the series by

CAROLYN KEENE

The Ghost In The Machinery
STEFAN PETRUCHA – Writer
SHO MURASE – Artist
with 3D CG elements and color by CARLOS JOSE GUZMAN
BRYAN SENKA – Letterer
JIM SALICRUP
Editor-in-Chief

ISBN 10: 1-59707-058-0 paperback edition
ISBN 13: 978-1-59707-058-4 paperback edition
ISBN 10: 1-59707-061-0 hardcover edition
ISBN 13: 978-1-59707-061-4 hardcover edition

Printed in China.
Distributed by Holtzbrinck Publishers.

10 9 8 7 6 5 4 3 2 1

NANCY DREW HERE, IN THE WOODS, ENJOYING NATURE, AND GRATEFUL TO WHATEVER CAVE PERSON HAD THE SENSE TO DISCOVER THAT WONDERFUL SOURCE OF HEAT WE NOW CALL FIRE!

UNFORTUNATELY, THIS CAMPFIRE DOESN'T HAVE LONG TO LIVE. I PLAN TO *MURDER* IT SHORTLY.

BRRR. NANCY, COULDN'T YOU HAVE PICKED A WARMER NIGHT TO ABSOLUTELY *INSIST* THAT WE GO CAMPING?

NANCY ISN'T HERE *JUST* FOR THE FRESH AIR. THERE ARE MUCH BETTER CAMPING SPOTS IN RIVER HEIGHTS, SO MY GUESS IS THERE'S SOME MYSTERY AFOOT.

I GUESS IT'S DARK ENOUGH NOW FOR MY *CONFESSION.* I READ IN THE PAPER THAT THE LOCALS HAVE BEEN REPORTING *STRANGE LIGHTS* IN THESE WOODS.

CHAPTER ONE:
I SEE THE LIGHT, BUT DOES IT SEE ME?

MOST WERE CLOSED AND FORGOTTEN DECADES AGO. THIS ONE WAS FORGOTTEN. SEEMS THERE WAS JUST TOO MUCH *PAPERWORK* AFTER THE SECOND WORLD WAR AND FOLKS WERE TOO BUSY CELEBRATING TO DO IT *ALL*.

WHEN SOMEONE BOUGHT THE PROPERTY THIS YEAR, THEY DECIDED TO LET THE NEW OWNERS PAY FOR DEMOLISHING IT. IT WAS SCHEDULED TO BE DESTROYED WITH EXPLOSIVES THE VERY NEXT DAY.

C'MON!

OH, NO! YOU'RE NOT THINKING OF GOING *IN THERE*?

THEY'RE BLOWING THIS PLACE UP TOMORROW!

THERE COULD BE *EXPLOSIVES* ALL OVER IT, SET WITH HAIR TRIGGERS!

BUT, BESS, WHAT IF THE *GHOST* IS MALE, FASCINATING AND SINGLE?

RIGHT, LIKE I'M GOING TO DATE A PSYCHO-KILLER GHOST!

SPEAKING OF WHICH, THAT'S *ANOTHER* REALLY GOOD REASON *NOT* TO GO OVER THAT FENCE!

HEY, WAIT FOR ME!

IT WAS BACK.

MY PALS, BESS AND GEORGE, DO *LOTS* OF THINGS ABOVE AND BEYOND THE CALL OF DUTY...

...AND I *OFTEN* LEAD THEM INTO DANGER BY MY OBSESSION WITH MYSTERY-SOLVING...

...SOMETIMES THE *REAL MYSTERY* IS WHY THEY HANG OUT WITH ME...

CREEEAAK!

AEEIIII!!

CRRAAAKKK

ESPECIALLY WHEN I GET SO WRAPPED UP IN SEARCHING FOR CLUES, THAT I *FORGET* WHERE I AM.

LIKE IN AN OLD, *ROTTING* BUILDING!

NANCY, GET A GRIP!

WE GOT YOU!

UH-OH...

SO, I'M AWFULLY GLAD THEY *DO* STICK WITH ME.

BUT I'M NOT SURE IT'S THE **SMARTEST** THING THEY COULD DO.

EEEEAAA!!!!

WUMPH!

OOF!

THUD THUD THUD

MAYBE FOLLOWING SOMEONE INTO DEATH-DEFYING ADVENTURES AGAIN AND AGAIN IS WHAT FRIENDSHIP IS ALL ABOUT!

UNNNK.

IN FACT, I WAS THINKING HOW **SWELL** THEY WERE, JUST BEFORE I PASSED OUT! I DON'T KNOW **WHAT** THEY WERE THINKING OF ME.

WHEN I OPENED MY EYES, I WASN'T SURE WHERE I WAS.

THERE WAS A LIGHT. ANOTHER LIGHT.

THE *PAIN* IN MY BACK MADE ME *DOUBT* IT WAS A LIGHT FROM BEYOND, BECKONING ME TOWARD THE AFTERLIFE.

BUT THE GHOSTLY HAND THAT REACHED FOR ME MADE ME WONDER IF SOMEONE FROM THE AFTERLIFE WAS PAYING *ME* A VISIT.

UNFORTUNATELY, THERE WAS ONLY ONE WAY TO FIND OUT.

AND I CAN'T *STAND* LEAVING A MYSTERY UNSOLVED!

IF HE WAS A *GHOST*, HE SEEMED FRIENDLY ENOUGH— LIKE CASPER, ONLY HEAVIER.

HELLO THERE!

GOOD THING I WAS HERE. YOU GIRLS WERE IN A BIT OF A *PICKLE!*

ALWAYS A *MISTAKE* TO VENTURE DOWN A RABBIT HOLE IF YOU CAN'T GET OUT YOURSELF! HA-HA!

WOW! CURIOSITY CERTAINLY GETS THE BEST OF *HER*, EH?

YEAH. NANCY RUSHES IN WHERE ANGELS... AND WELL, MOST *ANYONE*, FEAR TO TREAD.

WELL, *THAT'S* NOT GOOD!

BUMP
BUMP
BUMP

BUMP
BUMP
BUMP

THE PLACE TURNED OUT TO BE EVEN BIGGER THAN IT LOOKED. WE SEARCHED FOR *HOURS* THROUGH ROOM AFTER ROOM FILLED WITH OLD PIECES OF WAR TOYS.

ONE WAS LITTERED WITH PIECES OF PLANES LIKE THE *MUSTANG*, THE FASTEST FIGHTER IN THE SKY AND A VITAL TOOL FOR THE ALLIES BEATING THE NAZIS.

ROY WAS PRETTY SMART, BUT SOON HE LOOKED PRETTY LOST.

THE COMPASS IS SPINNING FASTER THAN A DERVISH AFTER A TURKISH ESPRESSO. WE *MUST* BE CLOSE TO THE TANK UNIT. HA!

AT LEAST ROY WAS *CHEERY* ABOUT THE WHOLE THING.

SKURNK

WHAT WAS *THAT*?!

PROBABLY A RAT. I HATE RATS! CAN'T WE JUST COME BACK DURING DAYLIGHT?

WE *COULD*, DEAR FELLOW, BUT THERE WILL ONLY BE DUST LEFT AFTER THE DEMOLITION!

P 02

HMMM. *THIS* IS INTERESTING. THE FLOOR IS DIFFERENT. NO MORE HARD-WOOD.

YES. THAT'S REINFORCED CONCRETE. STRONG ENOUGH TO HOLD UP... PERHAPS A TANK?!

SO LET'S FOLLOW IT...

RIGHT THERE WITH YOU, GIRL DETECTIVE! SOMETHING TELLS ME THIS LEADS RIGHT TO THE--

...IN **THERE!**

GOOD BET! THIS IS WHERE **I** COME IN HANDY!

I'VE READ ABOUT "HANDSOME HARRY" IN APB FILES...

THAT'S ALL **BEHIND** HIM, NOW! HARRY'S BEEN A CLEAN AND UPSTANDING CITIZEN FOR OVER THREE MONTHS!

CLICK

CLICK

QUIET DOWN OR I'LL LET YOU HAVE IT! UH... I MEAN, I WILL NEED COMPLETE **SILENCE**, IF YOU PLEASE!

CLICK

CLICK

I WASN'T SO SURE ABOUT HARRY. HE SURE SEEMED TO BE **ENJOYING** HIMSELF! AND HOW MUCH **HONEST** SAFECRACKING WORK WAS THERE?

I WASN'T REALLY PAYING ATTENTION TO WHAT WAS *RIGHT* BEHIND ME. NOT UNTIL IT STARTED GETTING *LOUD*...

YOU HEAR SOME-THING?

YES, I DO!

HEY, GUYS--

CAN'T YOU PLEASE BE--

END CHAPTER ONE.

I'VE BEEN ACCUSED OF BEING SO *FOCUSED* ON A MYSTERY...

HARRY! LOOK OUT!

I'VE *IGNORED* WHAT'S RIGHT IN FRONT OF ME...

WHAT THE... ?!

RRRUUUMMBBLLLE

SO I COULD *APPRECIATE* HOW INTENSE HARRY WAS ABOUT HIS WORK.

RRRUUUMMBBLLLE

BUT, YOU KNOW, THERE REALLY *IS* SUCH A THING AS BEING *TOO* FOCUSED!

CRAAASHHHH

CHAPTER TWO:
A CERTAIN MAGNETIC APPEAL

BUT, LOOKS CAN BE *DECEIVING* AND I FOR ONE HAVE ALWAYS FOUND IT EASIER TO *IGNORE* MY LITTLE ACHES AND PAINS...

...WHEN THERE'S A *MYSTERY* TO SOLVE.

HA! HA! HA!

SO I GUESS BEING *FOCUSED* REALLY IS A TWO-EDGED SWORD, MEANING IT CAN BE BOTH *BAD* AND *GOOD*, A *BOON* AND A *BANE*!

A-HA! HA! HA!

FUNNY AND, WELL, NOT SAD, BUT KIND OF WEIRD!

A-HA! HA! HA!

A-HA! HA! HA!

HEY, I'M GLAD TO BE ALIVE, BUT I DON'T THINK IT'S ALL THAT HYSTERICAL.

HA! HA! NO, NO, NO! THE GHOST DID US A FAVOR!

YOU SEE?!

HE WAS RIGHT. IT **WAS** FUNNY, ONLY I WASN'T LAUGHING BECAUSE I WAS TOO AMAZED!

HUGE PIECES OF THE CARRIER WERE **CLINGING** TO THE WALL OF THE VAULT!

UNGH! QUITE **STUCK**, I'D SAY!

BUT, WHAT DOES IT MEAN, ASIDE FROM A HANDY WAY TO DO CHIN-UPS?!

-UNGH- IT MEANS WE'VE FOUND THE TANK! IT **MUST** BE INSIDE THIS VAULT!

FAVOR? GUESS AGAIN! THE LOCK IS CRUSHED! I'LL NEED *POWER* DRILLS.

WE'LL HAVE TO GO GET THE GENERATOR!

WE CAN'T! IT'S GETTING NEAR DAWN! WE DON'T HAVE MUCH TIME!

NONSENSE! THERE'S *PLENTY* OF TIME FOR ME TO FETCH THE EQUIPMENT

AND FOR *ME* TO INVESTIGATE THE GHOST!

AND THE FUN WAS JUST BEGINNING...

GOOOO!!

THIS IS ONE GHOST THAT JUST WOULDN'T QUIT!

GEEEET OOOUUUT!

BUT I GUESS THAT'S HOW YOU GET TO BE A GHOST IN THE FIRST PLACE!

ERK!

I HAD LOTS OF QUESTIONS FOR THIS "GHOST." IN LIEU OF A SÉANCE, I OPTED FOR THE MORE *DIRECT* APPROACH.

YOU... MUST... NEVER... KNOW...

FUNNY, I DIDN'T THINK PAIN WOULD BE A BIG PROBLEM FOR GHOSTS.

WHAT HAPPENED?! DID HE GET *ACID* ON HIM?!

NO. THE BOTTLE IS STILL *SEALED*.

I WAS A LITTLE WORRIED ABOUT THIS GHOST HUNT MYSELF, ESPECIALLY NOW THAT I KNEW IT WAS A *LIVE* CRAZY MAN.

BUT, YOU KNOW, I WOULD NEVER HAVE SOLVED A *SINGLE* MYSTERY IF IT WASN'T FOR SOMETHING ELEANOR ROOSEVELT SAID.

WE HAVE TO LOOK FEAR IN THE FACE.

SO THAT'S WHAT I TRY TO DO, EVEN IF THE FACE OF FEAR IS SOMETIMES, YOU KNOW, *SCARY!*

LIKE WHEN YOU'RE STARING AT A TON OF *EXPLOSIVES* SET TO BLOW UP THE BUILDING YOU'RE STANDING IN!

YOU CERTAINLY TAKE US TO SOME *INTERESTING* PLACES, NANCY!

YEAH, NEXT OUTING, I'M PLANNING! MAYBE A NICE BOTTLE-CAP FACTORY THAT HAS *TOURS* SCHEDULED INSTEAD OF *DEMO-LITIONS!*

MEANWHILE, THE MEN WERE BUSY WITH BERTHA...

MAYBE WE SHOULD FORGET THIS AND GO HELP THE GIRLS!

NO! WE MUST REACH THE TANK WHILE THERE'S TIME! BESIDES, SOMETHING TELLS ME NANCY DREW CAN HANDLE HERSELF!

TRY NOT TO BREATHE!

≶COUGH≷ ≶COUGH≷ NO KIDDING.

MEANWHILE, ABOUT THE ONLY THING I DISCOVERED ABOUT THE GHOST WAS THAT HE WASN'T AFRAID OF *HEIGHTS*!

PART OF ME WANTED TO WALK UP AND *KNOCK*, BUT I DIDN'T KNOW *WHAT* THIS GUY WAS CAPABLE OF, AND I COULDN'T PUT MY FRIENDS IN THAT KIND OF DANGER.

CHEERING FROM BELOW TOLD US THAT BERTHA HAD DONE THE JOB!

YAY!

AT LEAST HE'S EATING RIGHT.

YOU KNOW, SOME SCIENTISTS SUSPECT EATING OUT OF ALUMINUM CAN GIVE YOU ALZHEIMER'S. MAYBE THAT'S WHY HE'S SO CRANKY.

COOL. BUT, WITHOUT ELECTRICITY, HE *CAN'T* BE GETTING GREAT RECEPTION.

THESE PHOTOS SHOW THIS FACTORY BACK WHEN IT WAS UP AND RUNNING.

GH-GH-
GHOOST...
H-H-HOME...
N-N-NOW...

I HADN'T EVEN HEARD HIM, WHICH WAS SURPRISING WITH ALL THE MUTTERING HE'D BEEN DOING EARLIER.

HE LOOKS SURPRISED FOR A MINUTE. I WASN'T SURE *WHAT* I COULD SAY TO APPEASE HIM.

UNFORTUNATELY, I FAILED TO COME UP WITH ANYTHING INTELLIGENT.

UH... HI?

WHILE WE WERE BEING CORNERED, THE MEN USED ALL THE STRENGTH THEY COULD MUSTER TO GET TO THEIR BOOTY.

AND THEY FINALLY HAD THEIR EYES ON *THEIR* PRIZE!

I'LL SHOW YOU TO MESS WITH ME AND MY STUFF.

WAIT YOU DON'T HAVE TO...

IT WAS JUST THEN, I FINALLY FIGURED OUT EXACTLY WHAT I WANTED TO SAY TO HIM!

BUT IT WAS TOO LATE!

END CHAPTER TWO

OUR STRANGE GHOST-FRIEND... NOT SO LUCKY.

YEEOOWW!

BUT I WAS STARTING TO FIGURE OUT *EXACTLY* WHAT HIS PROBLEM WAS.

NO! THEY *FOUND* IT! NO! MY *HEAD!*

MUST *STOP* THEM...

WAIT!

IN ALL THE EXCITEMENT OF OUR COUNTDOWN TO **DESTRUCTION** I'D ALMOST FORGOTTEN ABOUT OUR POOR DEMENTED GHOST MAN.

OOOOWWWW!

I COULDN'T BE SURE HE **KNEW** ABOUT THE DEMOLITION PLAN AND I DIDN'T HAVE MUCH TIME TO **WARN** HIM.

RATHER THAN DISTRACT ANYONE FROM THE TANK'S LIBERATION...

I FIGURED I'D HANDLE THIS **MYSELF**.

MOOAN

ONLY TO DISCOVER I WASN'T THE **ONLY** ONE TAKING MATTERS INTO MY OWN **HANDS**.

WHAT ARE YOU DOING?!

AFTER A FEW PRACTICE CIRCLES PROVED ME A **LOUSY** TANK DRIVER, I MANAGED TO AIM THE THING AT THE **DOOR**. BUT, I WAS CONCERNED ROY AND FELIX WOULD BE **INJURED** AS WE RIPPED THROUGH IT AND WHATEVER WALLS WERE BETWEEN US AND FREEDOM.

DON'T WORRY ABOUT A FEW BUMPS OR **BRUISES!** IF YOU **DON'T** GET US THROUGH THAT DOOR **NOW**, WE'LL ALL BE BLOWN TO **PIECES!** I SUSPECT **THAT** WOULD BE **WORSE**.

THE END

NANCY DREW HERE, DOWN AT THE STATION, BOARDING MILLIONAIRE RALPH CREDO'S *PRIVATE CHOO-CHOO* WITH ITS SPECIAL WOODEN CARGO CAR.

IT HAS TO BE *WOODEN* BECAUSE THAT TANK (WHICH I DROVE OUT OF THE OLD MUNITIONS PLANT BEFORE THEY BLEW UP THE PLACE, BY THE WAY) HAS AN ENGINE THAT USES DANGEROUSLY POWERFUL *MAGNETS*.

FELIX, A WAR VET WITH A METAL PLATE IN HIS HEAD, FOUND THAT OUT THE HARD WAY. NOW HE IS IN THE VETERAN'S HOSPITAL GETTING HELP.

CHAPTER ONE: TICKET TO HIDE

YOU'LL HAVE TO CONTENT YOUR-SELF WITH DENVER, MY FRIEND, WHERE *CREDO INC.* HAS THEIR RESEARCH FACILITY!

I'M GOING TO *STUDY* THAT ENGINE AND BUILD A MODEL STABLE ENOUGH FOR STREET VEHICLES!

WE'RE GOING TO *REVOLUTIONIZE* THE INDUSTRY, BROTHER! AND YOU CAN SAY YOU HELPED!

WHEN WE GET TO DENVER, RALPH WILL FLY YOU HOME! NOW, PERHAPS A *NAP* WILL IMPROVE YOUR DISPOSITION?

SLEEPING BERTH'S TO THE *REAR*, SITTING AND DINING UP *FRONT*.

ALL ABOARD THE CREDO EXPRESS!

THANKS, MR. CREDO! YOU'RE VERY NICE TO LET US COME FOR THE RIDE.

N'T MISS NANCY DREW GRAPHIC NOVEL # 10 – "THE DISORIENTED EXPRESS"

Go Undercover in Paris as Nancy Drew® in
Danger by Design

You, as Nancy Drew, are in Paris to work undercover for a prestigious fashion designer. Minette is all the rage in the fashion world, but strange threats and unwelcome guests are causing her to unravel. It's up to you to stitch the clues together and unmask the mystery in this PC adventure game.

dare to play™

FOR MYSTERY FANS
10 to Adult

Nancy Drew PC Adventure Game #14
Order online at www.HerInteractive.com
or call 1-800-461-8787. Also in stores!
Compatible with WINDOWS® 98/2000/Me/XP/Vista

Created by

HeR interactive

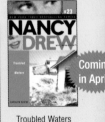

WATCH OUT FOR PAPERCUTZ

Papercutz Editor-in-Chief Jim Salicrup here with something really important to say to you before we kick off this edition of the Papercutz back-pages: Thank you!

Thank you for picking up this Papercutz book. Whether this is your very first Papercutz graphic novel or your second, third, fourth, or sixteenth—we greatly appreciate it. We work around the clock to make each and every one of our books the very best we possibly can, so that you can get the absolute maximum amount of enjoyment from each and every page. But it's all for nothing without you! And thanks to you, Papercutz has become quite a success story. We suspect that's because instead of offering more of the same types of comics that were already being published, Papercutz is devoted to bringing our own brand of fun and excitement to the world of graphic novels.

Thanks to you also for telling us what you like and don't like about Papercutz. That's been a huge help to us in choosing our new, upcoming Papercutz titles. By revealing how much you enjoy the humor in our mystery and adventure titles, such as The Hardy Boys, Nancy Drew, and Totally Spies, we knew our new series had to be just as much fun. We'll soon be adding a science fiction adventure series and a horror anthology to our line-up. And they'll both have that Papercutz sense of humor. One of the new titles is revealed on the very next page... But before you get to the big announcement, on behalf of all the Papercutz writers and artists, allow me to thank you one more time for giving us the opportunity to do what we love— create the very best comics we can for you!

Thanks,

JIM

Caricature of Jim drawn by Steve Brodner at the MoCCA Art Fest. Alien copyright © 2007 MARATHON-MYSTERY ANIMATION INC. "Team Galaxy" is a trademark of MARATHON-MYSTERY ANIMATION INC. All rights reserved.

What happens when three outrageous teenagers are thrown into the most eye-popping space adventures?

TEAM GALAXY tells the story of friends like no others: Josh, Yoko and Brett. The three of them have been chosen to attend Galaxy High, the coolest high school on earth, where they are trained to become space marshals. Throughout their adventures, the heroes of TEAM GALAXY will have to multitask between the tribulations of their teen lives and fighting the craziest alien villains ever known to man.

Don't miss this exciting new series, based on the hit TV series, seen on Cartoon Network and YTV, coming this Fall from Papercutz.

Now let's meet the stars of TEAM GALAXY...

Josh

With his leather jacket, motorcycle and crazy antics, Josh has earned the reputation of the rebel of Galaxy High. He prides himself on being a professional slacker, and always seems to be in trouble with the principal – who also happens to be his father. But for all his wild stunts, Josh's independent thinking is a perfect fit for the team.

Yoko

is a 15 year-old with a taste for the spotlight and funky fashion. Her wild streaked hair and colorful personality bring a unique element to the team. In addition to being amazingly talented (singing, dancing, writing, acting, playing guitar, painting), Yoko is a serious karate junkie, which helps when they have to battle with unsavory aliens.

Brett

is the youngest, and smartest, of the students at Galaxy High. With a fascination for gadgets and all things sci-fi, he is labeled a true brainiac. He can fix almost anything that goes wrong with the school's equipment – but just don't call him a "kid."

Nancy Drew (EMMA ROBERTS) in Warner Bros. Pictures' and Virtual Studios' teen drama action/adventure "Nancy Drew," distributed by Warner Bros. Pictures. Photo by Melinda Sue Gordon

The movie we've all been waiting for is almost here! To get a sneak peek, go online to: http://nancydrewmovie.warnerbros.com/ and watch the fun-filled, action-packed trailer plus a lot more. You'll get to see Nancy Drew in action, in lots of scenes from her soon to be released major motion picture!

The film follows Nancy (Emma Roberts) as she accompanies her father, Carson Drew (Tate Donovan), to Los Angeles on one of his business trips and stumbles across evidence about a long-unsolved crime involving the mysterious death of a beautiful movie star. Nancy's resourcefulness and personal responsibility are put to the test when she finds herself in the middle of the fast-living, self-indulgent world of Hollywood.

Top to bottom: Ned (MAX THIERIOT), Nancy Drew (EMMA ROBERTS) and Corky (JOSH FLITTER) in Warner Bros. Pictures' and Virtual Studios' teen drama action/adventure "Nancy Drew," distributed by Warner Bros. Pictures. Photo by Melinda Sue Gordon

Cast: Emma Roberts, Josh Flitter, Max Thieriot, Rachael Leigh Cook, Tate Donovan.
This film has been rated PG.

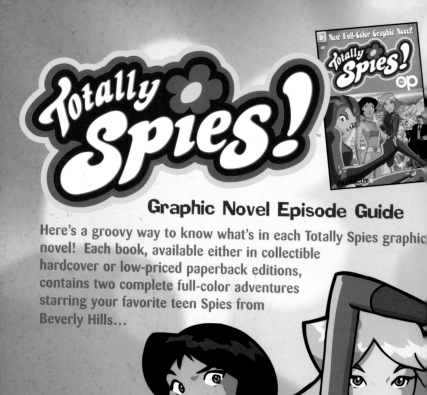

New Full-Color Graphic Novel!

Totally Spies! op

Graphic Novel Episode Guide

Here's a groovy way to know what's in each Totally Spies graphic
novel! Each book, available either in collectible
hardcover or low-priced paperback editions,
contains two complete full-color adventures
starring your favorite teen Spies from
Beverly Hills...

Totally Spies! Graphic Novel #1
"The O.P."

During a weekend road trip up the California coast, the girls' new car, a totally tricked-out, gadget-filled gift from Jerry to celebrate their recent success as super-spies, breaks down in a seemingly idyllic gated coastal town called Ocean Palisades – or "The O.P." for short. At first Alex, Sam, and Clover completely love it — the friendly, perfectly-tanned townspeople; the fancy, immaculate houses; the ridiculously scenic views – but, when they meet a few teens who seem to be too perfect to be real (they don't stay out after dark; they love spending time with their parents; they have sparkling teeth because they don't eat junk food), they start to get pretty weirded-out. Can the Spies find out what's really going on with the town's teens and save them from their crazy community – or will they be turned into perfect robot-like teens themselves and be forced to live in The O.P. forever?.

"Futureshock"

When the girls fiddle with Jerry's new time machine, they accidentally jet themselves 25 years into the future! At first they think it's way exciting – until they discover that Mandy is an all-powerful super villain who has control of all media! The spies are in awe when they see Mandy on the cover of every single magazine... starring in every single TV show and film... and dominating every single radio station – the whole time pushing her shallow Mandy agenda! And the worst part is, when the spies seek out their future selves, they discover that they're being held captive by Mandy! Desperate, present day Sam, Clover and Alex seek out future Jerry for help (he's the only one who knows how to work the time machine) — but to their shock, find that he's not exactly around anymore, he's had himself cryogenically frozen! The girls have to find a way to "thaw" him out, save the future versions of themselves from captivity, and stop Mandy before she totally "Mandifies" the planet!

Totally Spies!
Graphic Novel #2
"I Hate The 80s!"

Boogie Gus has updated his look a bit — unfortunately, not for the better. No longer a worshipper of the 70s, Gus has gleefully discovered the 80s. And he's bent on using his new device – "The Eightifier" to turn Beverly Hills into the ultimate 80s paradise. Can the Spies stop Boogie Gus before their home town goes retro for good? Can the girls deal with their complicated-to-maintain New Wave haircuts? Can they deal with all the synth-pop music at their school dances? Can they stop Jerry from wearing robin's egg blue sports jackets with the sleeves rolled up and pastel pink t-shirts underneath?!

"Attack Of The 50Ft. Tall Mandy!" It's time to crown the new Miss Beverly Hills. Among this year's hopeful contestants are Mandy and Clover. In order to get that extra winning edge, they both unwittingly decide to get a special full-body makeover that promises to make their hair, smiles, eyes and even their attitudes bigger. Mandy: "And everyone knows that bigger is better when it comes to this type of competition." But as they are getting their treatment, both strapped into separate full-body machines, a shadowy figure sneaks into the spa and puts a microchip into Mandy's machine. Mandy is suddenly growing bigger in every way. As the Spies start to investigate a rash of disappearances among Miss Beverly Hills contestants, they find out that Mandy, who has now grown nearly fifty feet tall, is behind the crimes. They also discover that along with becoming bigger physically, Mandy's meanness has also become magnified. And in an effort to win the competition, she decided to take out the other contestants. Can the Spies stop this monolithic Mandy menace before it's too late?

HELLO! IT'S NOT LIKE I *ASKED* TO BE TURNED INTO A FIFTY-FOOT TALL MONSTER LIKE YOU!

Totally Spies!
Graphic Novel #3
"Evil Jerry!"

Jerry's sinister brother Terence is at it again – and this time, with the help of Tim Scam, he's created a crazy device that has the ability to gather half of the evil from him... and transfer it directly into Jerry! Luckily, the spies start to notice that Jerry's acting strangely. And even luckier, they figure out what's going on – Terence and a troop of ex-villains are to blame! Yes, the girls finally discover the LAMOS! Can the spies save Jerry and WOOHP before it's too late – or will Terence proceed with the rest of his wicked plan – moving himself and the rest of the LAMOS out of their submarine and into WOOHP (from which they can spread their evil all over the world)?

"Deja Cruise!"

The spies are totally psyched when Jerry informs them that he's offering them a little vacation on the new WOOHP Cruise Liner – a state-of-the-art, luxury ship designed to be a pleasure boat for over-worked WOOHP agents! Once on the boat, the girls realize Jerry was-n't kidding, the ship is loaded with all sorts of amenities. Suddenly, the serenity of the vacation is broken as a gang of baddies, disguised as the ship's crew, take over the boat. Their plan: to destroy the ship with all of the WOOHP agents on it. The girls spring into action and try to defeat the villains, but their efforts only result in them acci-dentally causing the ship to sink. Or does it? The girls all wake up and find that things are back to normal. Was it all a bad dream caused by eating bad sushi? Suddenly, just as things seem to be back to normal, the entire incident happens again. The spies try to stop the villains, but again destroy the vessel. And yet, again, they wake up on the ship. The spies realize that they are re-living the same day over and over! And the only way to stop this vicious cycle is to defeat the bad guys. Can the girls figure out what to do, or will they be stuck on this boat forever?!

Totally Spies!
Graphic Novel #4
"Spies in Space"

The spies are way psyched when they find out that their favorite new band, The Alpha Centauris, are about to make music history. The band plans to be the first performers ever to broadcast a con- cert live from the moon. The only prob- lem is, it's just days before the gig and the band is nowhere to be found. Apparently, their space transport has completely disappeared from WOOHP radar. Jerry puts the Spies on the case (as if they would have it any other way) and after GLADIS outfits them with cool intergalactic gadgets, including awesome space suits, the girls head off to find the band. After finding their abandoned ship, clues

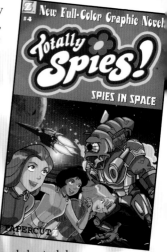

lead the Spies to believe the band was abducted by aliens. Can the girls save the band before they are evaporated by the sun?

"Spy Soccer"

It's the start of a new soccer season at Bev. High and Alex is psyched when her team gets a cool new coach. The only downside is that Clover and Sam feel a little snubbed because Alex is constantly busy with her team. Later, Jerry sends the girls on a mission to investigate a series of abductions. When the girls check out one of the crime scenes, they discover the place is totally trashed. And stranger still, one of the clues leads Sam and Clover back to... Alex?! When the girls confront Alex, she denies any wrongdoing, but can't explain or remember where she was at the time of the abduction. Then, seem- ingly out of nowhere, Alex's demeanor changes and she becomes very evil. She attacks Sam and Clover, and ultimately escapes. Sam and Clover discover that Alex's new soccer coach is using a special mind control ball to turn the Bev. High soccer team into her own private army – an army that uses their incredible, newfound, evil soccer techniques to get revenge on the coach's ex-teammates. Can Sam and Clover survive the final showdown – a death defying soccer match against the coach, Alex and her mind-controlled teammates?

The Hardy Boys in Comics
(and on TV and Vinyl)!

It's not that difficult to find an adult who remembers the late 70s live-action TV series, "The Hardy Boys Mysteries," with Shawn Cassidy and Parker Stevenson. And you can still find lots of Baby Boomers who recall the Hardy Boys serial, with Tim Considine and Tommy Kirk, which ran on the original Mickey Mouse Club TV series in the 50s. What's is almost impossible is finding anyone who might remember the Hardy Boys Saturday morning cartoon show from 1969. Like the Hardy Boys appearance on TV in the 50s, their animated TV series in the late 60s also inspired a four-issue comic-book series. But let's find out more about "The Mystery of The Forgotten Cartoon Series."

Back in the days long before entire cable networks were devoted to cartoons 24/7, the only place to see new cartoons on TV were on ABC, NBC, and CBS Saturday mornings. Back then Filmation Studios had a huge hit in the 60s with an animated series based on the Archie comicbook characters. Not only was it a hit on TV, but the songs performed by the animated Archies band became huge pop music hits — and you thought Gorillaz was the first cartoon band! But the technology didn't yet exist that could make it possible for a "cartoon band" to per-

form live on tour. The producers at Filmation decided to try to launch another cartoon series, based on characters loved by millions of children, but this time, they'd also assemble a live band made up of singers and musicians that looked just like the cartoon characters.

The Hardy Boys Gold Key Comicbook Checklist:

April 1970 – "Secret Of The Orinda Star," "The Dart-Riddle Rumble"
July 1970 – "Mystery Of The Catacombs," "Secret Mission"
October 1970 – "Mystery Of Wildcat Swamp," "The Headless Horseman"
January 1971 – "Paddle Wheel Peril" "The Guise Of Medusa"

The characters they chose to base this new show on was, of course, The Hardy Boys!

Filmation decided that in addition to solving mysteries, the Hardy Boys would be a touring bubblegum pop band. Joining Frank and Joe in this band, called The Hardy Boys Plus Three, were "Chubby" Morton, a character clearly based on Chet Morton, and new characters, Pete Jones (the first African-American character on a Saturday morning series*), and Wanda Kay Breckenridge.

For the non-singing parts of the show, actor Byron Kane provided the voices for Joe Hardy, Pete Jones, and Fenton Hardy; actor Dal McKennon did likewise for Frank Hardy and Chubby Morton, and actress Jane Webb supplied the female voices for Wanda Kay Breckenridge and Aunt Gertrude Hardy.

While the actual mystery/adventure stories were animated, the show did feature the groovy live-action band briefly at the end of each episode performing one of their songs. Two record albums were released, "Here Come The Hardy Boys" and "Wheels," featuring the musical Hardy Boys, and the first album even cracked Billboard's Top 200 Album Chart. About the only other place to "see" the live version of The Hardy Boys Plus Three was on the Hardy Boys comicbook's covers. Each of the four covers featured a mix of comic art and photos. The "live" band appeared most prominently on the second issue.

Oh, and the answer to "The Mystery of the Forgotten Cartoon Series" is that the show ran against the ratings blockbuster Scooby-Doo and everyone was watching the Scooby gang!

*While the prime time TV special, "Hey, Hey, Hey, It's Fat Albert," debuted in 1969 as well, "Fat Albert and the Cosby Kids" didn't become a regular Saturday morning series until 1972. Like The Hardy Boys it was also produced by Filmation Studios.